Peg Leg Pete and His Little Green Submarine

Written by James Adams

Illustrated by Nabeel Tahir

Independently published

Fort Pierce Florida

This book belongs to _____

Once upon a time, there lived a little boy named Pete. Pete lived on a small island and loved the ocean and everything in it. He spent all of his free time playing at the beach, reading about pirates, and dreaming about exploring the sea.

Pete loved talking about pirate adventures so much that his dad nicknamed him Peg Leg Pete. He daydreamed of all the adventures the pirates had and all the treasure they must have buried. All he wanted to do was explore the high seas!

One day, Pete's dream came true. His father, who was a shipbuilder, gave him a shiny green submarine as a birthday present. Pete was super excited. He couldn't wait to dive into the ocean and see all of its secrets.

Pete's little green submarine had all the newest gadgets and gizmos. It had a powerful engine, bright lights, and robotic arms that could pick up treasures and bring them to the surface.

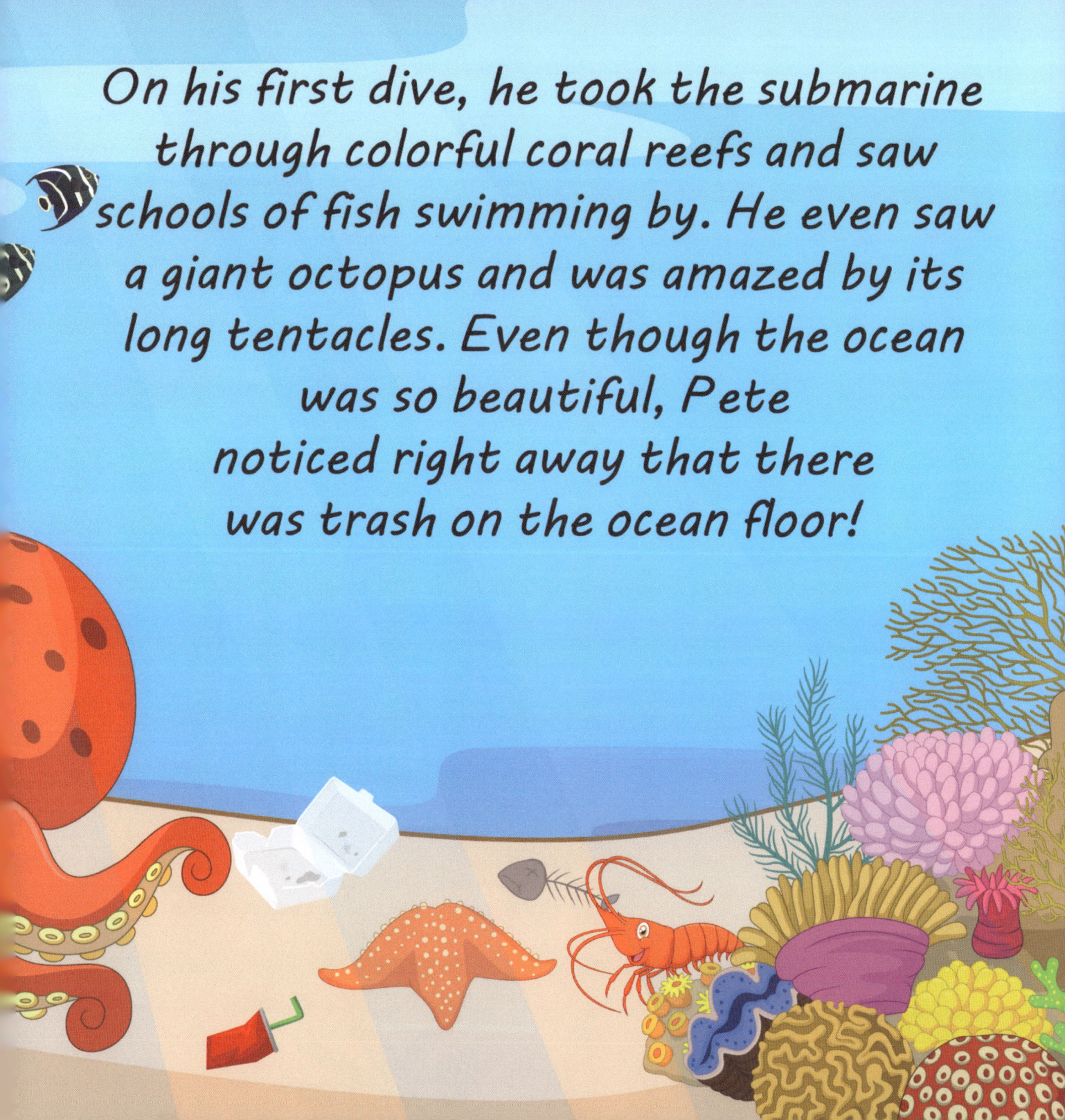

On his first dive, he took the submarine through colorful coral reefs and saw schools of fish swimming by. He even saw a giant octopus and was amazed by its long tentacles. Even though the ocean was so beautiful, Pete noticed right away that there was trash on the ocean floor!

During his dive, he found an underwater cave and decided to explore it. He carefully guided the submarine into the cave. The cave was so dark that he had to use the submarine's lights to see! After following the cave for some time, he spotted light coming from above.

He followed the light up and found a beautiful lagoon. He brought the submarine to the beach and anchored it. Something about this beach was strange and needed a closer look.

Pete jumped out of the submarine and saw jewels of every color twinkling in the sand. The jewels were different shapes, sizes, and colors. They were so shiny and pretty to look at. He could hardly believe his eyes!

He was so amazed by the lagoon that he didn't notice a group of sharks swimming towards him. Pete jumped in the submarine and chased the sharks away with the robotic arms. He felt so grateful and thankful for his new submarine.

Pete gathered all the jewels he could carry and took them home to his father. His father's eyes lit up when Pete showed him the jewels. "Wow, Pete," his father said. "Where did you find these?"

Pete said, "They came from a secret lagoon! I found them with my new submarine."

After that first adventure, Pete wanted his friends Mary and Jim to join him on his dives. They had so much fun exploring the ocean together and seeing new things. He loved taking his friends on adventures in his little green submarine and showing them all the amazing things the ocean had to offer.

Pete and his friends found shipwrecks and treasures. They saw trenches and underwater mountains. They found new types of fish and sea life that looked like aliens. They explored the ocean every chance they had.

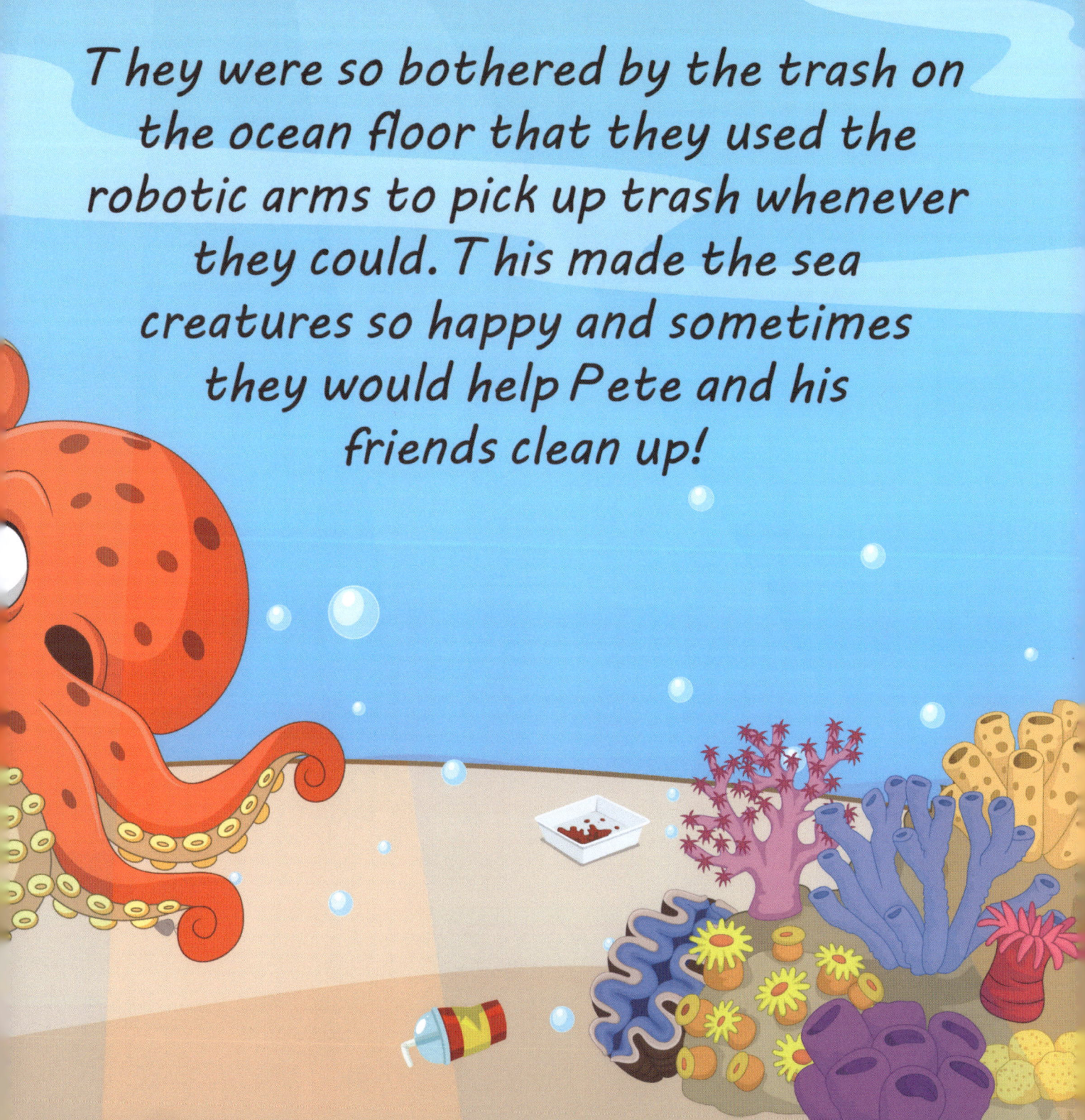

They were so bothered by the trash on the ocean floor that they used the robotic arms to pick up trash whenever they could. This made the sea creatures so happy and sometimes they would help Pete and his friends clean up!

Pete and his friends have plans to release an underwater picture book showing all the amazing things they have seen! Peg Leg Pete says "Ahoy" (that means hello or goodbye in pirate talk) and remember to keep a sharp eye out for the picture book. Oh, and please help keep our oceans clean!

Ahoy!
Thank You!

I really hope your child enjoys this book! It was fun to write and to think that it may spark the imagination of a child. If you enjoyed this book for your child, the best thing you can do is to consider leaving a review. I have included a QR Code to take you to your purchases in Amazon to make the process as easy as possible. Thank you again!

Printed in Great Britain
by Amazon